THE LONG-LOST SECRET DIARY OF THE WORLD'S WORST PIRATE

Book design by David Salariya
Illustrations by Sarah Horne
Additional cover illustrations by Ela Smietanka

Published in the United States by Jolly Fish Press, an imprint of North
Star Editions, Inc.

First US Edition
First US Printing, 2018

Library of Congress Cataloging-in-Publication Data (pending)
978-1-63163-141-2 (paperback)
978-1-63163-140-5 (hardcover)

Jolly Fish Press
North Star Editions, Inc.
2297 Waters Drive
Mendota Heights, MN 55120
www.jollyfishpress.com

Printed in the United States of America

THE LONG-LOST SECRET DIARY OF THE WORLD'S WORST PIRATE

Written by
Tim Collins

Illustrated by
Sarah Horne

JOLLY
FiSH
PRESS
Mendota Heights, Minnesota

Chapter I

Life at Sea

Wednesday, March 1st

Avast ye! I spy a bunch of scurvy dogs on the horizon. Raise the Jolly Roger and shiver me timbers!

Oh, who am I kidding? I'm not a pirate. I'm just a passenger on an ordinary merchant ship. And we're on our way to the port of Kingstown on the Caribbean island of Saint Finbarr, not sailing around in search of treasure. My life couldn't feel less like an adventure right now. But I did just climb up to the top of the mainmast. Sort of. I got a couple feet up the ropes before Dad spotted me and ordered me to come down. He's been like that ever since we set sail from England two weeks ago.

Because we're such important passengers, we're allowed to sleep in the captain's quarters at the back of the upper deck. Everyone else has to sleep in the crew's quarters on the lower deck.

I'm glad I don't have to sleep near all the stinky sailors, but I'm really bored of this tiny space. I wish Mom and Dad would let me out to look at the sea. I'm so sick of spending all day in my hammock listening to the wood of the ship creak.

Dad says the deck is too dangerous and I'll fall overboard and get eaten by sharks. He also probably thinks I'll throw up on everyone. Which I admit I did quite a lot when we first boarded. But I'd never been at sea before, and the constant swaying and dizziness took a lot of getting used to.

But that's all over now. I've got my sea legs. The chances of me ruining another barrel of biscuits by spewing in them are very low.

I'm back in my hammock now, dreaming of being a fearsome sea rover rather than a pampered passenger.

"Shiver me timbers," "heave to," and "pieces of eight," and whatever else it is pirates say.

Thursday, March 2nd

I snuck into the galley today and got our chef Noah to tell me pirate stories. I've never been at sea before, but everyone else has been sailing for years, and they've had loads of brilliant adventures.

Today Noah explained pirate punishments to me. He's told me before, but I enjoyed it so much I got him to go through it again.

As well as attacking other seafarers, pirates often fall out with each other, and the treatment they dish out is severe. Sometimes they maroon their victims on desert islands with just a pistol so they can shoot themselves with it if it all gets too boring. Other times, they whip their victims with a cat-o'-nine-tails, ripping open their flesh. And if they're really angry, they keelhaul them, which means they

tie their victims with ropes and drag them
across the rough underside of a ship. Ouch.

My least favorite of these would be keelhauling,
followed by the cat-o'-nine-tails, and finally
marooning. That last one doesn't actually sound
that bad. You could build yourself a shelter and
spend your days fishing and swimming. That's

got to be better than having your skin torn apart on the barnacles underneath a ship.

I have to put on a stern face when the others tell me stuff like this. I know it wouldn't be fun to be tortured, but the life of a pirate still sounds very exciting. Sometimes I think leading a boring, protected life is the worst punishment of all.

I'd love to go hunting for buried treasure. I thought that was what my life at sea would be like. I didn't think I'd be stuck here in my swaying hammock, writing my diary, and dreaming of something more exciting.

GET REAL

Marooning, keelhauling, and the cat-o'-nine-tails were all genuine pirate punishments. The cat-o'-nine-tails was a whip with nine knotted strands that could tear through flesh. It was made from a thick rope unraveled at one end. As well as giving agonizing cuts, it could spread diseases if the blood from the last victim hadn't been cleaned off properly.

Friday, March 3rd

Mom and Dad came into the captain's quarters to examine a map this afternoon. They were so distracted, I managed to sneak onto the upper deck and roam around. The sea was calm, which meant I could stroll about without any danger of falling overboard.

The ship didn't seem like such a bad place as I

wandered under the blazing sun and stared out at the endless blue ocean. I could only imagine all the pirates out there having brilliant adventures without me.

I stood behind one of the cannons on the starboard side and pretended I was a pirate firing on a passing vessel. I got so carried away that for a moment I thought I could really see another ship on the horizon, but I think I was just imagining it.

A breeze soon picked up and everyone began to stir. One of our crew members called Will shouted for help setting the topsail, which meant he wanted someone to climb up to the mainmast and unfurl a sail.

I offered straightaway. Will didn't look too keen, but before he could say anything I was dragging myself up the ropes.

14

The wind blew stronger as I went up, and the mast swayed back and forth. The ropes stretched and swung, making them really hard to climb. At times they shook so violently I had to grip them until my knuckles went white.

Finally, I reached the top and crept onto one of the horizontal wooden poles. I looked over at Will to see how he was untying his end of the sail. Then I made a big mistake. I glanced down.

The deck was much farther away than I was expecting. The crew was gathered around below. Two figures darted out of the captain's quarters.

Uh-oh. Mom and Dad.

I could see Dad's red face as I clung to the pole. I wanted to untie the sail and move calmly back down the ropes to prove him wrong for confining me to the captain's quarters. But I couldn't take my eyes off the deck.

The ship lurched wildly from side to side. I had this weird feeling that I was staying perfectly still and it was the ship and the entire sea that were swaying. Then I felt my grip loosening. I told my arms to hold on. But the motion of the ship made me queasy and my muscles were weak.

Wind whistled past me as I plunged down.

The next thing I knew, I was in Noah's arms. I could see Mom in front of me. Her face had gone pale. Somewhere behind me, Dad was ranting about how I could have been killed and this was exactly why I shouldn't have been allowed on deck.

Just my luck. I make one tiny mistake, and now he's going to go on about it forever.

Saturday, March 4th

Okay, so my attempt to climb up to the sails didn't go brilliantly. But I've apologized now and we should all move on.

No chance of that. Dad's still so angry he's forbidden everyone from speaking to me. Not only do I have to stay here in my hammock, but even if someone else came in, I couldn't get them to tell me pirate stories.

So I've just been lying here scribbling in my diary with my pencil and looking back over the other entries. One thing that's been on my mind is the ship I thought I saw when I was behind the cannon. The more I think about it, the more convinced I am that it was real.

I feel like I should warn the others, but how can I? I'm not allowed to speak to anyone.

Chapter 2

— ⊢—⊣ —

Mystery Ship

Sunday, March 5th

I did see a ship. I knew I was right.

I was meant to stay in the quarters again today, but I managed to sneak out just after dawn, while everyone else was still asleep.

I took the telescope from the captain's table and went out onto the deck. I stood at the exact place on the starboard side where I'd thought I'd seen the ship and gazed at the sea.

For a while I saw nothing but morning mist, but as it cleared I could make out a vessel in the far distance. It was another three-masted ship, just like ours.

A hand slammed down on my shoulder.

I turned to see our captain, who is called Joseph

Wright. At first he was really angry with me for taking his telescope, but he forgot all about it when I showed him the ship.

I returned to my hammock before Mom and Dad were awake, but all day I could hear conversations about the mysterious ship. I wanted to take credit for being first to spot it, but I didn't want to say anything in case Dad got angry with me for going out on deck.

All day people have been coming into the captain's quarters to look at the maps and discuss the progress of the ship. Apparently it's sailing right for us. I wonder what it wants?

Monday, March 6ᵗʰ

I'm writing this from my hiding place in the cargo hold at the bottom of the ship. There's a small gap behind the barrels of drinking water, and I made for it as soon as we were attacked. No one has discovered me yet. I don't want them to take me to the other ship. I want to stay here with the new crew.

This is where I belong now. This is my life.

There are plenty of hardtack biscuits down here, and I can survive on those and water until the time comes to reveal my presence to the others.

I was still confined to my hammock this morning. The arguments about the approaching ship were getting fiercer and fiercer. Mom and Dad wanted us to keep going for Saint Finbarr. Dad was keen to get started in his new job as governor, and he didn't want us to slow down for anything.

But Captain Wright thought the ship might

need our help. He said they might be lost or need vital supplies, and it was his duty as a fellow sailor to help.

Dad got really angry and said they could be pirates trying to trick us into stopping. I got so excited about this, I couldn't stay in my hammock anymore. I ran back onto deck, desperate for a glimpse of the salty sea rogues.

Dad and Captain Wright were so distracted by their argument, they didn't even notice I was on deck.

Captain Wright ordered the crew to shorten our sails so the other ship could catch us. Dad was screaming about pirates, and I watched the vessel approach, desperate for my first glimpse of the outlaws and their adorable parrots.

My heart sank. It wasn't a pirate ship. It was

just another ordinary merchant craft, like
Captain Wright had said. It was flying a British
flag, rather than a skull above crossed swords
or bones.

There weren't many crew members on deck, but
the ones I could see didn't look anything like
pirates. There was a man with a black hat and
a girl who was about my age. Neither had eye
patches nor wooden legs nor birds on their
shoulders. They waved and shouted as we got
closer.

Even Dad stopped saying they were pirates
now. Instead, he said the rest of their crew
had probably been wiped out by disease and
we'd risk catching it if we let them on. Captain
Wright took no notice and let the other ship
draw alongside us. I noticed that the vessel's
sails were quite badly torn, and the ship was
listing slightly to port side.

The man with the black hat said he'd lost his map in a storm and needed to check ours to see if he was on the right course. This sent Dad and Captain Wright off on another big argument about whether we should trust them.

While they were shouting at each other, I noticed two other crew members sneak out of their hold and fasten their ship to ours. They looked much shiftier than the man and the young girl. They had long, straggly hair and rough beards, and they were both missing a few teeth.

A loud crack rang out. That made Dad and Captain Wright shut up.

The man with the hat had a smoking flintlock pistol in his hand.

"Out you come, lads," he shouted. He fixed his gaze on Captain Wright and grinned. "Sorry about this."

Twelve men with thick beards and filthy faces rushed up from the lower deck. They were carrying pistols, swords, and axes.

GET REAL

Flintlock pistols were light weapons that pirates could easily carry with them when they raided ships. However, they weren't always reliable. They used flint to create sparks and ignite gunpowder to fire a metal ball at deadly speed. But they took a long time to load, and sometimes the powder would get damp and they wouldn't work at all. Some pirates carried more than one in a holster to save reloading time. Others would turn them around and use them as clubs once they'd fired them.

They were pirates after all. I wondered if they kept their parrots below decks while they were attacking ships.

"I'm afraid we need to exchange ships with you," said the man with the hat. "Ours has

sprung a leak. But you might be able to make it to shore if you hurry."

He lifted another flintlock pistol from his belt and pointed it at Captain Wright.

"You have a minute to get your crew onto our ship," he said. "After that, I'll lighten the load, starting with you."

I glanced over at Dad, expecting him to argue with Captain Wright again. But neither of them said anything. They just slumped their shoulders and traipsed onto the other ship. The rest of our crew followed.

I looked at the lopsided ship and wondered if it would ever reach land. We might find ourselves sinking below the waves before nightfall. But what choice did we have? An ordinary merchant crew like us would have no chance against a group of ruthless, bloodthirsty pirates. If we took their ship, we'd at least have some chance of surviving.

That's when I realized I did have a choice. I could go and hide while all the others were making their way onto the pirate ship. Then when we were a good distance away, I could leap out and demand to join the pirate crew.

So that's what I'm doing. No one spotted me rushing down to the cargo hold in all the confusion. Soon I'll come out of my hiding place and start my new life as a merciless sea dog. This is going to be brilliant.

Chapter 3

My Adventures Begin

Tuesday, March 7ᵗʰ

I might as well admit it. I'm still in the cargo hold.

The pirates only come down here for supplies every couple hours, so I've been able to sneak out and grab biscuits and water quite often.

I could probably get away with staying down here until we reach land, then try and find another ship to take me to Saint Finbarr. I'd be reunited with my parents if they managed to make it, and I could forget I ever wanted to become a fearsome outlaw.

The thing is, I can hear the pirates shouting and arguing above me and they sound quite scary. Instead of welcoming me into their crew, they might toss me overboard. I don't really have any pirating experience, so I won't be of much use to them.

No, I need to stop thinking like that. All pirates had to start somewhere. At one point they all had to ask someone to take them on and train them. It's not like they were born with treasure maps in their hands.

This is not the time for cowardice. I've always wanted to be a pirate. I'll kick myself if I don't take the chance now.

I might just eat some more hardtack
biscuits first, though.

Wednesday, March 8th

I didn't have to announce my presence to
the pirates in the end. I was caught stealing
a biscuit this afternoon. A member of the
crew called Ollie spotted me and brought me
straight up to the captain's quarters.

The man who'd been wearing the hat
was standing at the table and examining
Captain Wright's maps. He'd taken his hat
off to reveal long black curly hair. He looked
much more like a pirate now, although there
was still no sign of a parrot.

"We've got a stowaway," said Ollie. "Caught
him stealing supplies in the cargo hold."

I thought it was a bit rude of them to accuse me of stealing stuff when they'd just taken an entire ship. As the only remaining original passenger, I was technically the only one who *wasn't* robbing things. I considered pointing this out, but I suspected their reply would be to throw me overboard.

"Shall I give him the cat?" asked Ollie.

The pirate with curly hair looked up from his maps and stared at me.

The punishment didn't sound too bad. As a matter of fact, I'd been really missing our old cat, Geoffrey, as Mom had refused to let me bring him along. If they'd brought a kitty of their own onto the ship and they wanted me to look after it, that was fine by me.

Then I realized. He was talking about whipping me with the cat-o'-nine-tails. Oh dear. I needed to convince them I was a worthy pirate, and I needed to do it quick.

"Avast ye!" I shouted.

The pirate with curly hair looked at Ollie in confusion.

"Heave to!" I yelled.

"How many lashes should I give him?" asked Ollie.

"Hold off for now," said the pirate with curly hair. "This child could be useful to us. We can put him up on deck with George when we're approaching ships. We could do with someone else fairly normal looking. Give him a hammock in the crew's quarters and put him to work."

"Thank ye!" I said. "Shiver me timbers!"

The curly-haired pirate shrugged and said, "I'm sorry, son, but I have absolutely no idea what you're talking about."

GET REAL

"Shiver me timbers" is an expression of surprise made popular by Robert Louis Stevenson's book Treasure Island. *Timbers were the wooden support frames of sailing ships, and shiver means to shake. So a heavy storm or cannon attack could be seen to shiver the timbers of a ship. "Avast ye!" means pay attention. "Heave to" is a command to slow a boat down.*

Thursday, March 9th

None of the pirates talk like I was expecting, though some have strong accents and mumble a lot. It's just as well, I suppose. I only knew a few pirate phrases, so it wouldn't have been easy to communicate.

I've been given a hammock down on the lower deck, which is much more cramped than the captain's quarters. Captain Bartholomew, the pirate with the curly hair, has taken over those for himself. He seems fascinated with Captain Wright's maps, but I think he'll be disappointed when he finds out none of them have any buried treasure marked on them. They were just to help us get from England to Saint Finbarr.

I really hope that Mom and Dad and the others managed to make it there.

Our British flag has been taken down and replaced with one showing a grinning skull with bones behind it. Every pirate has their own design, made up of things like cutlasses and bones and bleeding hearts.

I went around introducing myself to the other pirates this afternoon. None of them were very friendly, and when I asked them to tell me stories about their adventures and sing bawdy songs, they ignored me. I'm sure they're fine once you get to know them.

GET REAL

You might think pirate flags always showed a white skull and crossbones on a black background, but there were many different designs. Some showed full skeletons, some featured bleeding hearts, and some flags were red rather than black. Not many original flags have survived, so we have to rely on descriptions in books.

Friday, March 10ᵗʰ

Captain Bartholomew handed me a piece of paper with a list on it this morning. Apparently it's his code, and all new crew members have to agree to it. The captain says that every pirate has to sign a set of rules when they join a ship.

These are ours:

I. All crew members shall be allowed one share of provisions.

2. Lights and candles must be out by eight o'clock.

3. Deserting in battle is punishable by death.

4. No fighting on board. All disputes are to be settled by pistol duels on shore.

5. Each crew member shall receive one share of any prize, except the captain, who shall receive two shares.

6. Any crew member who loses a limb shall be compensated with four hundred dollars.

7. Each crew member shall keep their pistol or cutlass clean and fit for service.

8. No crew member shall play at cards or dice for money.

9. Anyone caught stealing shall be given forty lashes minus one.

10. Anyone caught running away shall be marooned.

I couldn't believe the captain was shoving all these rules in front of me. Pirates are meant to live carefree lives of adventure outside the boring old law. You can't expect them to agree to even more restrictions than before. Even when Dad confined me to the captain's quarters, I was allowed to keep a candle burning after eight.

But I wasn't in any position to argue. And I'd already been caught stealing biscuits, so if anything I was lucky to have escaped the thirty-nine lashes.

I signed my name at the bottom, but I did it in a sloppy way so I could pretend that they forced me to if anyone ever put me on trial.

So that's it. I'm officially a ruthless pirate now. Even if I am a ruthless pirate with a very early bedtime.

topgallant

topsail

spanker

foresail

mainsail

Saturday, March IIth

I just tried to make friends with two of my shipmates Ed and Ollie. They were cleaning some cannons they'd brought onto our ship from their old one, and I offered to use my expert knowledge to help them. They told me they were coping fine.

Getting a close look at two of Captain Bartholomew's crew made me realize why he wants me to stand on deck as we're approaching ships. They don't have wooden legs or parrots on their shoulders, but even someone as trusting as Captain Wright would have guessed they're pirates.

Ed has wiry red hair and a huge fuzzy beard. Ollie has thin brown hair and a patchy beard. They are both incredibly dirty, with cracked, scabby skin. They are missing lots of teeth, and

their gums look very sore and swollen.
Dad told me that happens when you're at
sea for too long and you don't eat fruits
or vegetables.

We brought some lemons and limes with us
from England, but they ran out. As soon as we
find some buried treasure, I'll use my share to

buy fruits and vegetables. If I end up looking like just another smelly pirate, they won't need me to stand on deck as we approach ships, and I'll no longer be of any use.

GET REAL

Some pirates suffered from a disease called scurvy, which gave them swollen gums and sore joints. It's caused by a lack of vitamin C, which is found in fruits and vegetables. Some people still suffer from the condition today, though it's very rare. Most films about pirates leave out the scabby skin, loose teeth, and bleeding gums.

Chapter 4

Learning the Ropes

Sunday, March 12ᵗʰ

I noticed Captain Bartholomew studying a map
in our old quarters this morning, so I asked if
he needed any help finding treasure. He said he
had no idea what I was talking about and called
Ed and Ollie over from the deck.

"Ever used a cannon, boy?" he asked without
taking his eyes off the map.

"Er . . . yeah," I said. "I think I used one a few years ago, but I've forgotten exactly what I did."

"Ed and Ollie will teach you," he said. "We'll need all the help we can get next time we strike."

Ed and Ollie, muttering angrily to each other, led me to one of the cannons on the starboard side. Ed knelt next to the cannon while Ollie stood with his hands on his hips.

"Right," said Ollie. "When we do this for real, there'll be a whole bunch of us working together at top speed."

He handed me an empty canvas bag and a short piece of rope.

"That bag will be stuffed with gunpowder and that fuse will be lit," said Ed. "Use them

incorrectly and you'll find out why there
was a bit about losing limbs in the articles
you signed."

"Okay," said Ed. "Check the touchhole."

I examined the cannon. It was a long brass tube
on a wooden cart. There was a long piece of
wood with leather on one end next to it, along
with a pile of rags and a cannonball. There
were lots of ropes hanging off the cart, some of
which were fixed to the side of the ship.

I had no idea what a touchhole was, and I didn't
want to ask in case it made me look like I didn't
know what I was doing.

The only hole I could see was the large one on the front that the ball would fly out of. I lifted the cannon up and peered into it.

"The touchhole looks fine to me," I said.

Unfortunately, the ship listed violently to port side as I was doing this, and the weapon slid out of my grasp.

It slammed onto Ollie's foot, and he yelped with pain. He grabbed his foot and hopped about while Ed steadied the cannon.

"This is the touchhole," said Ed, pointing to a tiny gap on the top of the cannon. "If it gets worn, the whole thing can backfire."

It turned out that the big hole I'd been looking down was called the muzzle. You have to shove the bag of gunpowder down it, then push it in with the wooden pole. Then you have to wedge the wad of rags down, then place the cannonball in. Finally, you light the fuse, put it in the touchhole, and stand aside before it jolts back.

Ollie took me through all this really fast and expected me to remember it in the exact right order.

"Go! Go! Go!" shouted Ed. He pointed to the sea. "Imagine a ship is getting away from us and you need to fire now, now, now!"

I looked at all the stuff on the floor and desperately tried to remember what to pick up first. The rags, the fuse, the ball, the stick, the gunpowder bag, the ropes. None of them seemed right. I panicked and went for the fuse.

"Wrong!" shouted Ed. "That's a lit fuse. Remember, that comes last."

I screamed and threw it back down. Unfortunately it landed right on the small gunpowder bag.

"Ka-boom!" shouted Ed.

Hmm... I don't like the look of this one.

58

I'm no expert on explosives, but even I know throwing a lit fuse onto a bag of gunpowder isn't a good idea.

"Sorry," I muttered. I stamped on the bag, as if putting out a fire.

"There's a reason you wouldn't be able to do that," said Ollie. "You wouldn't have any legs left."

Monday, March 13ᵗʰ

I was looking forward to my next cannon lesson, but apparently I'm not going to get any more. Captain Bartholomew has decided it would be safer if I stayed away from them from now on.

Seems a bit unfair after just one lesson, but I'm sure they'll find something else good for me to do.

I spent the morning standing on deck and staring out at sea and watching for rich ships to attack. George, the girl pirate, came up to mop the deck, and I offered to help. But she refused to let me have anything to do with it, like she had to protect her amazing job from a jealous rival.

She didn't want to talk at all at first, but I asked her so many questions that she gave in.

She's been in Captain Bartholomew's crew since she ran away from home three years ago.

Whenever she has a break from cleaning, she gets the crew to teach her all about sailing. When she's older she wants to become a pirate captain with a crew of her own.

I said it must be weird to be a pirate and a girl, which she took the wrong way. I didn't say she shouldn't be both, but I just thought it must be odd to be surrounded by men all the time. But she wouldn't listen to my apologies and she refused to speak to me.

I hope I can make friends with George again soon because she's the only other pirate my age.

Tuesday, March 14th

Captain Bartholomew gave me a new job today.

He said I could be the assistant to Nathaniel, the crew's carpenter. I thought about how jealous George would be when she found out. Carpenter's assistant is a much more important job than cleaner.

Nathaniel is a little older than the rest of the crew. He has white hair and a thick mustache. You have to be a good pirate to survive that long, so I thought I could learn a lot from him.

I stood at the table in the crew's quarters while he showed me how to saw pieces of wood into plugs that could be used to fix leaks in the hull. He said he had to do it a lot in the last ship, but eventually the holes got too big and they had to swap vessels with us, which made me worry about Mom and Dad again.

He handed me one of his saws and a block of wood and told me to try it. I was convinced I'd mess it up, but I actually managed pretty well. I cut the wood into a long, tapered shape that could be hammered into a small hole. I didn't chop my fingers off or slice through the table or break the saw or anything.

Nathaniel turned the piece of wood over in his hands, nodded, and said it was fine.

I couldn't believe it. I'd actually found something on the ship I could do. I was finally going to become a valuable member of the crew.

Just as I was feeling like I was getting somewhere, Ed rushed down and announced that another crew member called Jeremiah had fallen from the rigging and shattered his foot. I wondered why he was wasting time telling the ship's carpenter about this instead of trying to help the poor fellow.

"Fetch him here," said Nathaniel. He grabbed his biggest saw and cleared space on the table.

That's when I realized. Nathaniel wasn't just the ship's carpenter. He also was the ship's doctor. It made sense. Captain Bartholomew didn't need a full-time doctor on his crew, and Nathaniel already had all the saws.

Nathaniel handed me a bucket and pointed to the end of the table.

"I'll lay him out with his broken foot on that end," he said. "You hold his leg still and collect the blood and the foot. Toss it all overboard as soon as we're finished. It will stink the place up if you leave it to go rotten."

I felt my stomach flip over as I pictured the bucket with a severed foot in it.

There was the sound of a man's screams getting closer. Jeremiah was on his way.

The bucket shook in my hands as I tried to hold it in place at the bottom of the table. I told myself it was all going to be fine. I didn't have to saw through any bones myself. I just had to hold his leg in one hand and the bucket in the other and collect the shattered foot and the spurting, spraying, splattering blood.

The next thing I knew I was on the upper deck staring into the bright sun.

"I've never had an assistant faint before the surgery even started," said Nathaniel. There were splashes of blood in his white hair, and his shirt was stained deep red. "It was quite a nasty one, too. You should be glad you missed it."

It turns out I'm not so brilliant at being the assistant to the ship's carpenter/doctor after all. The search continues for something I can actually do.

GET REAL

Not many pirate crews contained a dedicated doctor. So if someone needed emergency medical help, the ship's carpenter often was called in. After all, if he could saw through wood, flesh and bone would be no problem.

If one of your limbs was infected or crushed, the easiest thing to do would be to take the whole thing off. The carpenter would saw through it, then burn the bloody stump with a red hot poker. You might lose a limb, but you'd gain a greater share of the ship's earnings, or a one-off payment, depending on the terms of your articles.

Wednesday, March 15th

I found another pirate who would speak to me today. His name is Samuel, and he's the only one on the ship with dark skin. He was captured and forced to be a slave, but he escaped when the ship that was taking him

from Africa to the Caribbean was wrecked. He managed to swim to a desert island, where he met up with Captain Bartholomew and his crew. They were marooning a sailor called Saul who'd been caught stealing, and they were happy for Samuel to take his place.

Samuel was mending a ripped sail on the port side of the deck. It looked like quite an easy job compared with the ones I've tried so far, but he refused to let me help. Not that he needed any. His hands were moving so fast it looked like the sail was mending itself.

Samuel was happy to tell me about the different types of sail, but when I asked him about when he was enslaved, he went quiet.

Mom once told me about what horrible lives slaves have, so I probably shouldn't have mentioned it. I was just trying to make conversation.

GET REAL

One of the most famous black pirates was known as Black Caesar. He served on Blackbeard's ship, The Queen Anne's Revenge.

Thursday, March 16th

Captain Bartholomew has finally found a job for me. Sadly, it's not a very exciting one. I have to go to the bottom of the cargo hold, scoop the water that's gathered there into a bucket, traipse back up, and fling it overboard.

Sometimes when waves crash over the side of the ship, the water gets stuck in the lowest part of the ship, which is called the bilge. There's a pump that's meant to get rid of it, but ours isn't working very well, so I've been given the job of taking the extra away.

If too much bilge water collects it can sink the ship, so I've got quite a heroic job really, when you think about it.

It doesn't feel very heroic, though. The water is really smelly, and lots of rotten bits of food have ended up in it. According to Captain Bartholomew, I'll need to keep my wits about me because sometimes rats end up in there.

Maybe I should have tried harder with the amputations. Even collecting severed limbs in a bucket sounds better than getting attacked by rats.

Friday, March 17th

No bilge duty for me today. Captain Bartholomew has spotted a merchant ship and we're planning to attack tomorrow. We're going to use the same tactic of pretending we're an ordinary ship until we get close. I'll be joining George on deck as we approach and doing my best to look needy.

Captain Bartholomew has been observing the ship through his telescope, and he doesn't think it's as good as our current one. So this time we're going to steal as much as we can and bring it back onto this ship.

Luckily, I've been put on stealing duty rather than fighting duty. Don't get me wrong. I'm sure I'll be brilliant at hand-to-hand combat eventually. But I need to build my confidence up gradually. I don't want to go straight into battle on the first attack.

Chapter 5

⊢——⊣

My First Battle

Saturday, March 18th

We approached the ship early this morning. I stood next to George on the quarterdeck and put on my best pleading stare. The ship slowed down for us, just as Captain Wright had done.

This other ship was smaller than ours, with just two masts. The sails looked like they'd been repaired a lot, and some of the yards looked wonky. I could see why we didn't want to steal it.

Captain Bartholomew waved his hands and shouted for help. At first it worked, but something must have made them suspicious when they were just a few feet away because they lowered their sails and tried to get away. I hoped it wasn't because my helpless expression hadn't been convincing enough.

Captain Bartholomew yelled for the others to come out. There was no point in hiding now. Samuel ran over to the flagpole, lowered the British flag, and raised our pirate flag.

Our crew raced onto deck, and Ed and Ollie handed everyone ropes with grappling hooks on the end. They lobbed them into the rigging of the other ship until there was a tangled web linking us.

They all began to drag on the ropes, and I joined in. I grabbed one with both hands and yanked it back as firmly as I could. I probably didn't make a massive contribution to reeling the ship in, but I felt like I was doing my part.

As the ship drew nearer, Samuel lit the fuse of a large wooden ball and lobbed it over. It landed on their deck with a loud explosion and thick

smoke spread everywhere. Their crew yelled in panic as Samuel kept on throwing more balls.

I now know these balls were grenades filled with a mixture of gunpowder, rags, and tar. I'm glad they didn't give me the job of throwing these. Samuel only had a couple seconds between lighting and throwing them if he wanted to keep all his fingers.

Ollie lobbed small metal spikes onto their deck as the thick smoke spread. I could hear the cries of the sailors as they threw themselves down to escape the explosions.

Captain Bartholomew lowered a wooden plank from the starboard side of our ship onto theirs. He drew his cutlass and rushed into the smoke. Ed, Ollie, and the others on battle duty followed him. I hung back with George, Nathaniel, and a couple of the others.

Every so often, a gap in the smoke would clear and I'd see a flying fist or swinging cutlass. I saw Captain Bartholomew firing his flintlock, then turning it around to bash one of the sailors on the head.

I heard slashes and screams from the smoke, then Captain Bartholomew telling us to climb on.

George stormed down the plank and I tried to follow her. But I felt it shift beneath my feet, and I had to stop and throw my arms out to the sides just to keep balance. I could hear the others behind me telling me to get a move on, and then I made the mistake of looking down at the waves.

My legs went weak. I felt like I had when I had fallen down from the sails. Only this time I wouldn't crash down into the arms of someone on deck. I'd splash into the sea, no doubt to be scoffed by a hungry shark.

I wobbled left, I wobbled right, then I felt my feet being swept out from underneath me. I clenched my eyes shut.

It didn't feel like I was plummeting down. I opened my eyes again and saw that Nathaniel was carrying me onto the other ship. He lugged me over the deck and into the captain's quarters.

"You search in here, and I'll try the cargo hold," he said.

He set me on the floor and dashed away before I could thank him.

I ran around the cabin, looking for the treasure.

There wasn't any hidden under the pile of clothes in the corner or inside any of the hammocks. There wasn't a single gold coin or precious jewel in the whole cabin. I just hoped the others were having more luck.

There was a large pile of maps on the table. If I couldn't find any actual treasure, I could at least find out where some was buried. I sifted through the whole pile, looking for a desert island with a big "X" in the middle. But all I could find were boring trade route maps.

I heard Captain Bartholomew calling us back. So much for my treasure hunt. I grabbed a compass from the desk and rushed out. It was better than nothing.

The crew rushed back across the deck, and this time I made it over the plank with no problems.

I was still scared of falling in, but I was much more frightened of getting caught by the sailors we'd robbed.

George and the others piled onto our deck behind me. It looked like none of them had managed to find any treasure either. No one was carrying any chests or jewels. They were clutching piles of cloth, medical potions, and barrels of food. It made me feel a lot better.

When we were all back on the deck, we cut the ropes tying us to the other ship and let our sails down. Samuel kept throwing his grenades at their quarterdeck as we moved off, trying to stop them from coming after us to get revenge.

The sailors should be pleased they escaped with their lives. Not many people meet a bunch of ruthless pirates like us and live to tell the tale.

Someone from the other ship fired their flintlock at us. The shot went wide, but I realized it might be a good idea to get off the deck.

I tried retreating to the crew's quarters,

but found that Nathaniel was setting up his surgery for those wounded in the battle. I decided this might not be a great place to relax either.

In the end, I went down to the cargo hold and watched the bilge water swaying from side to side. It was strangely relaxing after such a stressful day.

GET REAL

Pirates used early versions of grenades that were balls made from iron or wood filled with gunpowder. Rags and tar could be added to give off smoke and make things more confusing for the enemy. The metal spikes were known as caltrops. They had a triangular design that meant one of the sharp points always landed upward. Sailors usually had bare feet, so this was a simple and painful weapon.

Sunday, March 19th

We gathered in the crew's quarters this morning while Captain Bartholomew examined the loot we'd taken. To my surprise, he was pleased with all the others for taking stuff like cloth and medical supplies. But my contribution didn't go down very well. There were sniggers from the rest of the crew as I showed my compass to the captain.

"That was all I could find," I said. "I looked everywhere, but I couldn't find any treasure. I even checked for maps of desert islands, but the only ones I could find were of trade routes."

"Idiot!" shouted Captain Bartholomew. "Those are exactly what we want! If we know where the trade routes are, we know where to attack merchant ships."

"But why bother with all that boring stuff when you could dig up some treasure instead?" I asked. "We'd never need to attack another ship again if we found an entire chest full of gold."

"What are you talking about?" asked the captain. His face was bright red. "No one leaves money lying around in the ground! If you want to stay on my ship, start living in the real world."

I was sent to my hammock, and I wasn't even allowed to eat any of the food the others had plundered. They said I wasn't allowed my share because I didn't perform my duties properly. Nathaniel took pity on me this evening and gave me a hardtack biscuit, so at least I didn't go totally hungry.

I wasn't that sad about missing out on boring food anyway. I was more upset that our

captain had no interest in searching for buried treasure. That was the bit I was most looking forward to about being a pirate.

GET REAL

Although pirates search for buried chests of gold and jewels in stories such as Treasure Island *by Robert Louis Stevenson, it didn't happen very often in real life. Pirates were much more likely to divide their money up and spend it straightaway than bury it in a secret place.*

Real pirates were more interested in trade maps than treasure maps. Trade routes could direct them to ships loaded with valuable cargo such as spices or cloth.

Chapter 6
Pirate Haven

Monday, March 20th

I found out something very exciting today. I'm going to be on dry land again soon. Captain Bartholomew has decided to take us to a small town called Port Anthony that's known as a haven for pirates, where we'll be able to stock up on supplies.

It's going to be so strange to be on land again. I've been at sea for five weeks now, and I've forgotten what it's like to have solid ground beneath my feet.

I hope the pirates I meet in Port Anthony are more like the ones I was expecting, with one-of-a-kind slang, rowdy songs, and talking parrots. Maybe I can switch to a different crew and go off hunting for treasure like I wanted to do in the first place.

GET REAL

Pirate havens were ports where the authorities left seafaring criminals alone. They could sell stolen goods, recruit new members, and stock up on essentials. Some of the most famous ones were Port Royal in Jamaica, Barataria Bay in America, and Tortuga, a Caribbean island that now forms part of Haiti.

Tuesday, March 21ˢᵗ

Stepping onto land again was just as weird as I expected. When I first boarded our ship, it took me ages to get used to the movement of the boat. Now being somewhere that wasn't lurching from side to side felt just as odd. I found myself swaying as I walked.

Port Anthony was a maze of shacks spreading

from the beach up to the surrounding hills. I saw hundreds of pirates sitting outside bars and drinking from pewter tankards or haggling with store owners as I staggered around.

I accidentally bumped into a man with a red beard who was sitting on a barrel and he accused me of drinking too much grog. I told him I'd never even tried it, but he just laughed. Judging from his breath, he'd tried it a lot.

The pirates in the haven looked pretty much the same as the ones on my ship, with straggly beards, dirty faces, and missing teeth. But a few of them looked more like the sort I was hoping for. I saw one man with a huge black beard twisted into pigtails with ribbons in them. I wanted to find out if he also spoke like a proper pirate, but when he fixed his small black eyes on me, I was too frightened to speak. I suppose the man wanted to look scary, and it

97

must help him when he's threatening people. But it made me glad the pirates on my ship are actually quite normal. I reckon ribbon-beard man would do more than banish me to my hammock if I messed up.

I was just getting used to dry land again when I spotted Ollie, who was carrying a huge barrel. He said we were getting ready to leave again, so I followed him back to the ship.

On my way, I found a trader who was happy to swap my compass for a bag of limes. It's just as well because when I got back on the ship, I found that nearly all the others had bought nothing but grog. Nathaniel had bought some barrels of biscuits, Samuel had bought some rope, and Captain Bartholomew had managed to find some trade maps, but the rest of them had only bothered to stock up on the disgusting

drink. If you ask me, that was hardly worth
going all the way to a pirate haven for.

GET REAL

*Grog was the name for a mixture of water
and rum that was popular on ships. Water
can taste horrible when it's been stored
for too long, so many sailors added rum
to make it drinkable. To stop sailors from
arguing over shares of rum, it was mixed
with water before it was given to them.*

Chapter 7

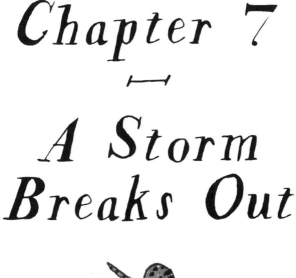

A Storm Breaks Out

Wednesday, March **22**nd

Things have gotten very rowdy on the ship
since they bought that grog. Instead of getting
on with their duties, the crew sat on the deck
for most of today shouting at each other.

At least it gave me another chance to talk to
George, as she's the only other one who isn't
interested in the stuff. She says the crew

always gets sloppy when they've got a fresh store of grog, but she doesn't mind because it gives her a chance to try out some different jobs.

She let me help her today, and I feel like much more of a proper sailor now. She showed me which ropes to pull to control the sails. It really made my arms ache, and sometimes the ropes passed so quickly through my hands that my palms felt like they were burning. She also taught me how to secure the ropes by tying different kinds of knots. The more the rest of the crew drank, the less they cared about their duties, and soon we were pretty much running the ship.

Now I'm glad the others wasted all their money on grog. It's given me my best training as a seafarer yet.

Thursday, March 23rd

I was helping George with the sails again this morning when a storm broke out.

Thick black clouds blew over and strong winds whipped against the starboard side of the ship. We began to sway as strong waves swept across the deck. Heavy rain lashed down and everything went dark.

George rushed down to the crew's quarters. Over the noise of the rain, I could hear her yelling. She returned on her own.

"I can't wake any of them up," she said. "It must be the grog. We'll have to prepare the ship on our own. Help me with the sails."

She clambered up the ropes and I followed. I tried to forget what had happened last time I climbed them. That had been a reasonably calm

day and I'd still managed to fall off. Now I had to do it in a high wind and there would be no one to catch me.

At the top of the ropes, George ventured onto the yard and tugged up the topsail. I reached out and helped her tie it. It was lucky she'd given me the lesson about knots the day before. We scurried back to the deck. The shortened sails helped us cope with the winds, but the huge waves were still rolling us around madly. The ship plunged up and down so fast I found myself slamming into the deck. I was amazed the others were managing to sleep through this.

"We've taken on too much water," said George. She rushed over to the pump and heaved the handle up and down.

"Don't worry!" I shouted. "I'll get my bucket." This was the moment all my bilge water

training had been leading up to. I ran down the stairs, managing to stay on my feet as the ship shunted me from side to side.

I grabbed my bucket and took it down to the bottom of the ship. The bilge water was so high it almost came up to my knees. I filled it with water and ran back up the stairs, as more foaming waves washed down.

There was no way I could remove the water faster than it was coming in. But I had to try. If we took on too much water, we'd sink.

I emptied my bucket over the side of the ship.

"That's not going to be quick enough!" shouted George. She abandoned the pump and ran to the barrels of grog on the starboard side. She picked one of them up. "We need to lighten the load or we'll sink."

"You can't get rid of those," I said. "That's the grog!"

"It's a choice between grog and death!" she cried.

"I think the others would still choose grog," I said.

"Well they're not here, so they don't get a say!" she shouted.

She tossed the barrel over the side.

I wanted nothing to do with this. There wasn't anything in the pirate rules about wasting grog, but I expected the punishment was getting whipped, keelhauled, and then marooned.

I continued removing the bilge water with my

bucket while George tossed the precious grog over the side.

Luckily for us, the storm calmed down as quickly as it had swept in. With my brilliant bucket skills, I could now remove the water faster than it was coming in. After just a few hours, the bilge water was almost back to its old level.

It was around this time that the others finally stirred.

Ollie stepped up onto the deck, looked at us in confusion, then ran to the port side and threw up.

"Thanks for helping us in the storm," said George.

Ollie's only reply was another burp.

110

Soon all the crew were on deck too. One by one, they found a free space on the side of the ship to lean over and throw up.

It was pretty disgusting, but I suppose I should be grateful they aimed their sick over the side of the ship rather than letting it flow into the bilge water. That would have made my job unbearable.

Friday, March 24th

After all the drama of yesterday, the sea's been totally calm today. I wish I could say the same about the crew.

As soon as they discovered that George had gotten rid of their precious grog, they got really angry with her. Then she got annoyed with them for being ungrateful and went to her hammock to sulk. I did warn her they'd rather drown than lose their grog.

I felt like I should defend George, but I didn't think the crew would listen to me, so I went to see Captain Bartholomew instead.

I found him in his quarters studying the map he bought in the pirate haven. I explained how George's quick thinking had saved everyone, and suggested he explain it to the crew.

To my surprise, he agreed. He gathered everyone on deck and demanded they all apologize to George individually.

Some of the crew looked annoyed, but Captain Bartholomew managed to lift their mood by talking about the next attack. He said his new map has loads of trading routes marked on it, and the merchant ships would be easy pickings for us. He said we'd be able to steal so much valuable stuff, they'd never run out of grog again.

The crew let out a massive cheer at this, which I thought was odd. Don't they remember how sick the grog just made them? Or do they enjoy being sick? It's very strange.

Anyway, the captain's speech did the job, and every single member of the crew went downstairs to apologize to George. A few of them even thanked me too, which I wasn't expecting.

I almost feel like I'm becoming a proper pirate after my shaky start.

Saturday, March 25th

I don't know why the crew was so upset about losing their grog. Things have been much better

since George got rid of it. Everyone has been doing their duties properly, and no one has been barfing over the side.

I finally got through all the bilge water this afternoon, so I hung around with George and got her to go through some more of the stuff she's learned about ships.

She showed me a way of calculating the speed of the boat using a plank of wood on the end of a knotted rope. You throw the plank into the sea and count how many knots go through your hands before the sand in a glass timer runs out.

I love learning all this stuff, and I bet it will come in use one day. If the next lot of grog the crew buys is even stronger, George and I might have to run the ship on our own for weeks.

114

GET REAL

Sailors worked out the speed of their ships using a wooden board tied to a rope with knots at regular intervals. They'd count how many knots passed through their fingers in a fixed amount of time, and use this to calculate their speed. The unit for measuring the speed of a boat is still called a knot, which is equal to one nautical mile per hour. Although modern methods are more advanced, the term dates back to a time when sailors made clever use of simple equipment.

Chapter 8

We Head Into Battle Again

Sunday, March 26ᵗʰ

Today should have been my most glorious
day ever as a pirate. But it doesn't feel
very glorious.

We made good progress all morning, and we
soon reached one of the trade routes marked
on the captain's map. It turned out to be
accurate. Within an hour, we'd caught sight of a
merchant ship.

We went through our usual routine, with
George, Captain Bartholomew, and me on
deck pleading for help while the others hid
below. But this time the ship didn't fall for it
at all. A distant figure on the deck looked at
us through a spyglass, then sped away in the
opposite direction.

Captain Bartholomew called the crew up right
away and we pursued them. Our sails were in

better condition than theirs, and we were soon able to get right alongside them.

The crew gathered around one of the cannons on the port side.

"Run out!" shouted the captain.

Samuel emerged from the lower deck with a cloth bag of gunpowder. Ed and Ollie and four of the others hauled the cannon over to the gunport in the side of the ship. Samuel shoved the gunpowder into the muzzle, followed by some rags and the cannonball. Ollie picked up the long wooden stick and pressed it all down.

Captain Bartholomew placed a spike down the touchhole to pierce the bag of explosive.

The crew hauled the ropes until the end of the cannon was sticking through the gunport.

Captain Bartholomew stuck a lit taper into the touchhole, and there was a deafening crack. The cannon shot backward, straining at its ropes.

I found myself cowering behind my hands, but I don't think anyone saw. They were all looking at the other ship and cheering. The cannon had smashed right through their hull.

We fired three more times, and hit them each time. Samuel added to the attack by lobbing grenades.

The merchant ship was now listing to starboard. Captain Bartholomew slammed down a wooden plank from our deck to theirs and charged across it. The others cheered and followed.

I felt someone tapping me on the shoulder. George was holding out a cutlass for me. I grabbed it with my trembling hand.

This was the moment I'd been waiting for. My chance to feel like a proper pirate and charge into battle. But I couldn't make myself do it. I didn't care if I got marooned for running away. I didn't want to attack anyone.

I dropped the cutlass, sloped down to the hull, and crouched in the bilge water. I shoved my fingers in my ears so I couldn't hear the screams coming from the other ship.

Our crew soon piled back on with the bags and barrels they'd taken from the other ship. I slid out of my hiding place and helped them store their plunder. No one asked where I'd been. My disappearing act must have gone unnoticed in all the confusion. I was hoping to hear the voices of the crew of the merchant ship as they were marched onto our ship, but they never came. That means we left them on the ship we destroyed.

I really hope they manage to find an island or another ship before they sink. I know I'm not meant to care about our victims, but I can't stop worrying. Drowning must be really horrible, and they didn't do anything to deserve it. They were just ordinary sailors.

I hope this doesn't mean I'm a coward. You can't be a pirate and a coward.

Monday, March 27th

I wonder if there's a way to be a pirate without actually attacking people. Maybe I could just threaten to hit them if they don't give me their stuff, and back down if they refuse. I'm not sure

that will win me a reputation as a fearsome outlaw of the sea, though.

The more I think about it, the more I think pirate life might not be for me. I don't want to harm anyone, I don't want to risk my life to steal boring things like spices and cloth, and I definitely don't want to drink any disgusting grog.

Maybe I should have gone onto the other boat with Mom and Dad and tried to make it to Saint Finbarr.

Tuesday, March 28th

There's a huge fight going on because some of the crew wants to go back to the haven and sell their plunder right away, while the others want to attack more ships first.

Captain Bartholomew settled it. We'll go after one more merchant ship before returning to the haven. He said the ships might abandon the trade route when word gets out that pirates are patrolling it, so we should take advantage now. On the other hand, if we plunder too much it will make our ship dangerously heavy.

It's impressive how quickly Captain Bartholomew can end arguments. One minute, they look like they're about to fire their flintlocks at each other. The next, everything is back to normal. George always stops to watch him in these situations. I think she's picking up tips for when she's in charge of a crew herself.

So it won't be long before we're back on the attack. I really hope no one notices me sneaking down to the hull again.

Chapter 9

Pirate Hunters

Wednesday, March 29th

I haven't been able to update my diary for a while, and I'm struggling to remember exactly how it all happened.

I might as well try. I've got plenty of time to think about it now. For all I know, I could have forever.

The first day I need to fill in shouldn't be too hard. It was pretty eventful, to put it mildly.

We spotted the ship early in the morning. Captain Bartholomew got George and me to stand on the deck with him as usual, while the others waited below.

The merchant ship slowed for us. It looked like this was going to be an easy attack.

But as we approached, I got the sense something wasn't right. There were only four crew members on the deck. They were clean-shaven and wearing neat white shirts.

I wondered if they were playing the exact same trick on us as we were playing on them. They'd get near, ask for help, then release a crew of pirates from below. We'd have two sets of bloodthirsty outlaws going head to head, and that wasn't going to end well. I doubted I'd be able to get out of that by hiding in the cargo hold.

It turned out to be even worse.

Everything seemed quiet and calm as we sailed over to them, but I couldn't shake the idea that something awful was about to happen.

Captain Bartholomew shouted that we'd lost

our way and needed to look at their maps, and the captain of the other ship said he'd be happy for him to step aboard.

We drew alongside their ship, and their crew members bound our vessels together with rope.

Captain Bartholomew jumped onto their deck, drew his cutlass, and shouted to the others to come out.

Our crew dashed up from below, but so did theirs.

They weren't pirates. They were wearing white trousers, blue jackets, and blue hats.

This was a Royal Navy ship. A ship full of pirate hunters.

The sailors leapt onto our deck and charged

at us with their swords raised. More and
more piled up from the lower decks. We were
outnumbered.

I tried to rush down to the cargo hold, but one
of the sailors grabbed my arms and hoisted
me into the air. He carried me over to the
navy ship and up to their quarterdeck.

The sailor slammed me down and tied my
wrists and ankles together. I tried to struggle
against my bonds, but soon gave up. I realized
I'd need my energy if the others overpowered
the navy and set me free, so it would be better
to hold still.

There was a loud explosion. At first I thought
we might have hit the navy ship with a
cannon. Then I realized that wouldn't be very
good news for me. I was bound in rope on

135

their quarterdeck. I'd go down with it if it sank. Smoke rose up from the deck. It wasn't a cannon I'd heard at all, but one of Samuel's grenades. Maybe things would be okay after all.

I squirmed around on the slippery planks, desperate to get a view of what was going on. I wriggled around to face the bow of the ship, but I still couldn't see anything happening below.

Eventually I heard someone coming up the stairs. I was hoping it would be one of our crew members ready to cut my ropes away and take me back to our ship.

It was someone from our crew—Ollie. But he was being lugged up by one of the sailors, just as I'd been. The sailor slammed him to the deck and fastened his hands and feet together. Ed, Samuel, Nathaniel, and George followed.

136

I could still hear swords clanging on the
deck below us, and I held out hope that our
remaining fighters would triumph over the
navy. But when they carried the captain up too,
I knew it was all over.

Soon everyone was on the quarterdeck,
squirming against their restraints.

After a while, they took us all back to our
ship and dumped us on the floor of the crew's
quarters, still with the tight rope binding us.

It made sense. A bunch of navy pirate hunters
were hardly going to abandon a perfectly
good ship. They were taking us and our vessel
back to land.

They left us until late that night, when one of
them came in to feed us stale biscuits and stale

water. Even then they didn't untie us. They just poured the water into our throats and shoved the biscuits into our mouths.

We stayed there all night. Eventually everyone got so exhausted from struggling against their ropes that they fell asleep.

GET REAL

Navy fleets patrolled the seas searching for robbers. This led to some legendary showdowns between pirates and pirate hunters. In 1718, naval officer Robert Maynard tracked down and killed Edward "Blackbeard" Teach. Blackbeard was said to have been shot five times and stabbed twenty times. Maynard chopped his head off and hung it from his ship.

Thursday, March 30th

My second day as a prisoner was the worst. I woke up with an itch on my right thigh. I tried rubbing it against the planks, but that just made my whole leg sore.

My back and neck ached from being tied up.
Our empty hammocks were swinging above us.
I wondered why they hadn't offered to lift us
onto those for the night.

Then I remembered. We were the bad guys.
We were criminals, being taken to shore for
punishment. We didn't deserve any comfort,
and we didn't deserve any mercy.

The others started talking about what would
happen to us, and I got really scared. I'd never
have become a pirate if I'd known the penalties
were so harsh.

Ed said that instead of taking you to jail, the
navy made you dance the hempen jig. At first I
didn't think it sounded too bad. I'm not brilliant
at dancing, but I was willing to try if needed.

But as the others discussed it, I realized what

they really meant is that we'd be hanged.

The rope is made of hemp, so it looks like you're dancing as you flail around on the end of it.

Ollie said they'd hang us as soon as we reached the docks, and that huge crowds of sailors would gather round and applaud. They all hate pirates, so they love to watch their enemies die. They even leave your body to rot on the gallows as a warning to anyone who thinks becoming a pirate is a bright idea.

After a while they bury your face down on the shore, to make sure you don't get into heaven. I found this especially unfair as I thought I'd have a much better chance of getting into heaven than the others. All I've really done is steal a compass. I was sort of hoping they'd let me off for that at the pearly gates.

I was still worrying about this when Captain Bartholomew spoke up. He said the ones who got hanged were the lucky ones. Some pirates are locked into iron cages and hung up to starve.

Every time I drifted off to sleep, I dreamed I was dangling in a dockside cage with sailors jeering below me and gulls pecking at my flesh.

GET REAL

Pirates were hated by the sailors they preyed upon, and their public punishment drew huge crowds. Some were brought back to London's Execution Dock to be hanged. Their bodies would be left on the riverside gallows until the tide had washed over them three times.

I'd wake up, realize the dream wasn't true, feel relieved, then remember I was a prisoner of the navy on my way to certain death, and feel stressed again.

Friday, March 31ˢᵗ

As time went on I thought of something that made me hopeful. Was I actually a pirate at all? Except for stealing the compass and visiting the haven, I hadn't done much to count as one. I'd signed the articles of agreement, but they could easily have forced me to do that.

When the sailor came that night to give me my biscuit and water, I tried to explain.

"There's been a mistake," I said. "I'm not really a pirate at all."

I could hear the others muttering angrily

143

behind me. I was glad they were tied up so they couldn't keelhaul me.

"Of course not," said the sailor. He had a scar down the right of his face and a couple small bloodstains on his white shirt. "I bet none of you lot are. This has all been a big mix-up."

He tipped his water bottle into my mouth, but I was so keen to talk that I spat it out again.

"They are, but I'm not," I said. Some of the others were hissing at me now. "My dad's the governor of Kingstown. These pirates took over our ship."

"You don't look like a governor's son to me," said the soldier.

"That's because I've been tied up for the last

three days," I said. "But look at my teeth." I opened my mouth and drew my lips back. "I haven't got scurvy like the rest of them."

"Traitor!" shouted Ed from the back of the deck.

"Spoiled little brat!" cried Ollie. "You can't go crying to daddy now."

This did a better job than anything I could have said. The soldier folded his arms and stared at me. I kept moving my mouth around to show him my healthy teeth and gums.

"Nah," he said, shaking his head. "A governor's son wouldn't be on a boat like this."

He shoved the biscuit in my mouth and stomped off.

The others jeered behind me as I crunched the biscuit.

When I'd finished, I craned my head round to look at them.

"I was going to rescue you all if he freed me," I said. "That was my plan."

The others kept scowling.

"We'd all have done the same if we were you," said George. "There's no need to lie."

I felt myself blushing. I shuffled over to the far side of the quarters, getting as far from the others as I could. Even with their arms and legs bound, they could still shuffle over and kick me if they wanted, so I thought it would be better to stay away.

My desperate pleading hadn't gotten me released. It had only turned the others against me. Now I'd die feeling like a traitor as well as an outlaw.

Chapter 10
—
Going Overboard!

Saturday, April 1ˢᵗ

I stayed in my spot at the side of the crew's quarters for most of the fourth day. I hoped that the others would forget all about my pathetic attempt to escape if I stayed out of sight.

I found myself thinking of all the changes that had happened since I'd been on the boat. First merchant sailors had been in charge, then pirates, now the navy. And it had all happened in the same few square feet of creaking, floating wood.

I only left my spot to shuffle toward the door to get my ration of water and biscuits that evening.

When I'd finished, I dragged myself back to the edge of the cabin and felt a sharp stabbing pain in my palm. I looked over my shoulder and saw that one of the plugs Nathaniel had used to fix

151

the hull had splintered apart. A wedge of wood was sticking out of the hull, and I'd accidentally embedded a chunk of it in my hand.

I was cursing my bad luck when something occurred to me. There was a piece of wood sticking out from behind me that was as sharp as a knife. Maybe even sharp enough to cut through rope.

I rubbed my wrists up and down on the wood, shoving more splinters into my skin. Each one added to the agony, but I didn't care. My rope was fraying and I felt real hope for the first time in days. I stopped to check that the others weren't looking at me. But they were all staring at the sailor who was shoving one of the hardtack biscuits into Captain Bartholomew's mouth.

I dragged the rope back and forth along the splinter again and it snapped loose. After four days of hell, I was free. I could stretch my arms, I could scratch my nose, I could take out all the soldiers with devastating punches and steer the ship back to freedom. Well, maybe not the last one, but a nose scratching was definitely in the cards.

But I found myself staying completely still. I didn't even pick the splinters out of my hands.

If the others saw I'd gotten my hands free, they'd insist I untie them too. Then there'd be a bloody battle against the guards, which I might not survive. And even if I did, and we managed to get control of the ship back, we'd only sail off and attack other ships again. And I really didn't want to go back to that.

I just wanted things to be safe and normal again. And something told me that a fight to the death with the navy wasn't the best way to achieve that.

So I stayed hunched against the side of the ship with my arms behind my back as if they were still bound.

Even after the sailor had finished giving everyone food and water and they went to sleep, I lay totally still, unsure of what to do.

I was pretty sure my next step should be to untie the ropes around my legs. But then what?

Go upstairs to the sailors and try to explain things again? No, they'd just think I was trying to overpower them and they'd rush at me with their swords.

Jump overboard and swim for it? No, we could be

days from land. Even without ropes on my arms and legs, I'd drown.

When I was sure the others were all asleep, I stretched my hands round to pick the splinters out. It was fiddly work and almost impossible in a dark, swaying cabin.

I was so focused on it, I didn't notice George waking up.

"What are you waiting for?" she hissed. "Untie us all!"

I lifted my finger to my lips. I was worried she'd shout and wake the others up, but she managed to stay quiet. She shuffled over until she was right next to me.

"I can't decide what to do," I whispered. "I don't want to get into a massive fight with the

guards, and I don't want to be a pirate again. But I don't want to stay on this ship and end up getting hanged, either."

George pulled herself upright and thrust her wrists toward me.

"At least untie me!" she said. "Then we can decide what to do."

"Okay," I said. "If you promise not to wake everyone else up."

"Promise," she whispered.

I pulled at the knot around her wrist until it gave way. George shook her hands for a few seconds and started on the ropes around her ankles. I did the same on mine.

"So what should we do?" I asked.

"Find somewhere to hide on the ship," she said. "We can escape when they get to shore. Where did you hide when we first took this ship over?"

"In the cargo hold," I said. "There's a space between the water barrels and the hull."

"Okay," she said, getting up. "Let's head there."

She crossed the cabin without making a sound and tiptoed up the stairs. We'd have to go up to the deck and down again to get to the cargo hold.

My feet were full of pins and needles after being tied for so long, and I couldn't stop myself swaying. The planks made much more noise when I stepped over them, and I was terrified of waking someone up.

When I reached deck, George was almost at the cargo hatch. I tried to tread lightly, but my numb right foot buckled and sent me crashing down.

One of the sailors came rushing out of the captain's quarters.

"Prisoners!" he shouted. "They're escaping!"

George pelted over to port side, then to starboard. She paused and peered into the gloom.

I dashed over to her.

"What now?" I asked.

"I think I can see land," she said. She pulled herself up onto the side of the ship.

I stared in the direction she was gazing, but I could only see dark sky and dark ocean.

"How sure are you?" I asked.

The sailors were piling out of the captain's quarters now. Some of them were carrying cutlasses.

"Not very," she said. "But it's worth a try." George jumped off the side of the ship. A moment later, I heard a splash.

I turned to the advancing sailors.

"I can explain!" I said. "My ropes accidentally came off and I was trying to find you so you could give me some replacement ones."

One of the sailors thrust his cutlass ahead and charged.

I had a split second to choose between drowning and being stabbed. It wasn't the nicest choice I'd ever made.

My stomach flipped as I realized I was about to jump. It wasn't really something I could avoid. A sharp knife was heading toward me, and I needed to escape.

I must have pulled myself over the side and plummeted into the water, but I'm finding it really hard to remember that bit.

The next thing I knew, I was in a dark and silent world with salty water filling my nostrils. Then I was above the waves again, struggling for air, then underneath them again, then above them again.

George was ahead, pulling herself forward. She

seemed to know what she was doing, so I swam after her.

The water blurred my vision and made the cuts on my palms sting.

I kept swimming, trying to blink the sea away so I could see George. I told myself that if we

kept going, we might reach land. Maybe George only saw a patch of seaweed or a reflected cloud, but she could have seen a shoreline. It was possible.

Then my mind played a horrible trick and reminded me the sea was full of deadly things like sharks and jellyfish and monsters. After that, I kept imagining my hands and feet were hitting sharp teeth and blubbery tentacles.

Eventually my foot did touch something. I wasn't imagining it. I wondered if I'd just kicked a shark in the nose and it was about to drag me to the depths of the sea. But my other foot also hit something solid.

We'd reached land.

I wiped my eyes and looked ahead. George was

standing on a beach and watching me with her hands on her hips.

"Told you I could see it," she said.

I scrambled out of the waves and collapsed onto the sand. I spent the rest of the night there, drifting in and out of sleep.

George stayed awake, keeping watch for the ship. But the navy never came after us.

Chapter II

—

Marooned

Sunday, April 2nd

That brings us up to yesterday. As soon as the sun rose, we went off to explore. It didn't take long. The beach surrounds a high, rocky clump covered in palm trees. We climbed and saw jagged stones on the other side, leading down to the sea again.

So it turns out we're on a desert island. We're marooned, but by accident rather than for punishment. It's better than being whipped or keelhauled, and it's definitely better than being left in a cage on the docks to starve.

There's a small spring of fresh water running down from the hill, there are plenty of coconuts, and we've come across no dangerous wild animals so far. In other words, we should be able to stay alive until we can get the attention of a passing ship.

But how long will that take? Weeks? Months? Years? I have no idea if we're still near any trade routes.

After we'd explored the island, George went off to build us a shelter from wood and leaves while I dried my diary in the sun one page at a time.

Aah... I could get used to island life.

Monday, April 3rd

That brings me up to today, most of which I've spent writing this.

It's very peaceful here on the beach in the morning sun. The waves are lapping at my feet, and I can hear distant bird cries. I know we're in massive danger, but it doesn't feel like it.

We still don't have any idea where we are. George has climbed to the top of the tallest tree, and she couldn't see any sign of another island or ship. So we're probably not near any trade routes.

Never mind. At least we've got food and drink. Right now I'm sipping spring water from an empty coconut shell, and it's much nicer than the stuff we had on the ship.

In the meantime, I must try to avoid asking George too many questions. She's building a separate shelter so I don't wake her up in the night and ask her if lions and tigers live on desert islands.

She's going to keep the current shelter, which is on the south end of the hill, and I'm going to take the new one, which is under the trees on the north side. It looks like she's putting it as far away as possible, but I don't really mind. I'm quite looking forward to having my own place after all that time on the crowded ship.

*Tuesday, April 4*th

Boredom is a big problem on a desert island. The only thing I have for entertainment is this diary. I'm glad I wrote it in pencil rather than ink because I can still read my old entries now that the pages have dried out.

It's keeping me entertained, though it's a little annoying to read all that early stuff about wanting a more exciting life. Look where it's gotten me. Stuck on an island where the best entertainment I can hope for is an interestingly shaped cloud.

It was like a dream come true when we were attacked by pirates. I thought my new life of adventure was about to start. Now I wish they'd left us alone and we'd sailed on to Saint Finbarr as planned. If I ever make it there, I promise I'll never moan about my life being unexciting again.

Wednesday, April 5th

What was I thinking? Why did I ever complain about being bored on a desert island? I completely forgot these places always have buried treasure.

So now I'm off to find some. I've got a wide piece of bark that will do as a spade, and I'll keep digging until I find a buried chest. Then when a ship comes to take us to land, we'll be rich. Even if I can't find my parents, I'll still be able to afford a massive house, and George can come and live there too, so she won't have to be a pirate anymore.

Thursday, April 6th

Brilliant news! I've found the treasure!

I dug into the rough ground beneath the palm trees on the north side and found a wooden chest. I pried it open to discover it was stuffed with gleaming coins and jewels.

I've spent all evening watching my treasure glint in the bright sunlight. It's so bright and

shiny. Everything's going to be okay. All our problems are over.

☠

Friday, April 7ᵗʰ

I showed the treasure to George last night and she pointed out that it wasn't actually treasure at all, but rather a pile of old coconut shells.

I think I might have gotten a little confused yesterday. I stayed out in the boiling sun too long without drinking water. By mid-afternoon, my brain was so fried that I mistook a pile of shells for valuable loot.

173

George has now banned me from treasure hunting, and she's ordered me to sit next to the spring and drink water until I feel better.

I knew the whole treasure chest thing was too good to be true.

Saturday, April 8th

George has managed to light a fire using dry sticks. This means we can eat cooked food as well as coconuts. She gave me a sharp stick and sent me into the sea to spear some fish. I splashed around in the water all morning, chasing the shoals that flitted around my feet. But every time I jabbed at them, they disappeared.

George came over to check how many fish I'd caught, and I had to admit I hadn't gotten any.

Without saying a word, she thrust the stick down into the water and pulled it up to reveal a flapping, skewered fish.

So that's what we had for dinner. Well, she had most of it, which is only fair because she caught it. But she let me eat the head and tail and a couple of the other bits she didn't want.

Fish leftovers and coconut might not sound like the best meal in the world, but it's a lot nicer than slimy water and stale biscuits.

GET REAL

Many seafarers were marooned on desert islands, but some managed to survive for years. Alexander Selkirk was a Scottish sailor who spent the years between 1704 and 1709 as a castaway on an uninhabited island in the South Pacific Ocean.

He survived by eating feral goats and made clothes from their skins. He built two huts from the trees on the island, using one for sleeping and one for cooking. A British ship finally rescued him in February 1709.

Selkirk was the inspiration for Daniel Defoe's classic book, Robinson Crusoe. *Defoe's fictional castaway survives for almost thirty years, and befriends Friday, a man he names after the day they meet.*

Sunday, April 9th

I wish I could make fire like George does. I tried striking bits of wood together for hours this afternoon, but they wouldn't burst into flames.

When it gets dark, George lights a fire outside her shelter. I asked her to do the same near mine, but she refused. She's still annoyed with me for talking too much.

I've thought of a good way round it, though. I'm going to build a stack of dried leaves outside my shelter and steal some of her fire tonight.

Monday, April 10th

Just as I planned, I took a dry stick over to George's shelter last night and set fire to it. I carried it back to my pile of leaves and they soon erupted into a wonderful blaze. My drab

shelter instantly transformed into a cozy, bright home. It reminded me of our old fireside on a winter evening.

I imagined I could see pictures in the flames, and it was the best entertainment I'd had since we arrived on the island.

I'd meant to enjoy it for an hour or so and then put it out, but the heat made me very drowsy. I lay back in my hut and decided to rest my eyes for a couple minutes. I went to sleep straightaway.

I had a dream where the navy sailors were tying me up again. Except this time they were putting the ropes around my throat rather than my hands and feet. I was back on the ship, but on a really hot day. Hotter than any I'd known before.

I opened my eyes to find the air thick with black smoke.

After a fit of coughing, I sprang to my feet. Bright orange flames were raging outside my shelter, and I had to leap through them with my hands over my face.

It was obvious what had happened. My small fire wasn't so small anymore. It had engulfed the dry leaves on the ground and spread to my shelter.

George was not going to like this. My shelter would burn down and I'd have to ask her to build me a new one. Plus, I'd have to admit to stealing her fire.

I was still fretting about this when the flames leapt up to the trees above my shelter.

This was not good. If the fire spread over the whole island, I'd have much bigger things to worry about than George's temper. I needed to wake her and ask what to do.

I dashed along the path to her shelter.

Halfway along, I came to a halt. There was someone there. It wasn't my imagination again, like the treasure chest. We were no longer alone on the island.

A dark figure far too tall to be George was charging down the path toward me.

"We saw your sign," said a man's voice.

I could make out the outline of his overcoat as he stepped closer.

"My sign?" I asked. I couldn't remember making

a sign. I'd been meaning to spell out "HELP ME"
in coconut shells on the beach, but I was sure I
hadn't got round to it yet.

Then I remembered. The north of the island was
on fire. That would count as a pretty major sign.

"Of course!" I said. "My sign."

It began to sink in. Not only had we been found
by a passing ship, but I also could pretend I'd
burned my shelter on purpose. My behavior had
gone from idiotic to heroic in an instant.

"You made the right choice in stopping for us," I
said. "My dad's a powerful governor in the port
of Kingstown on Saint Finbarr. He'll give you a
huge reward if you take us there."

"Come back to the ship," said the man. "You can
tell the captain about it."

Chapter 12

⊢—⊣

Back on Dry Land

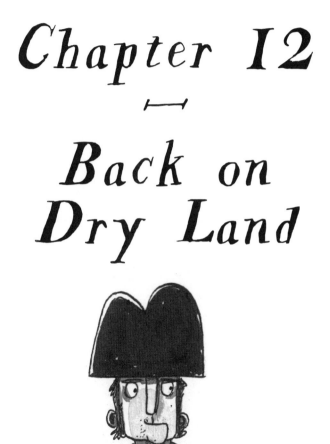

Tuesday, April 11th

I'm writing this from the deck of another merchant ship. The captain has agreed to take us to Saint Finbarr for one hundred dollars.

I have no idea if my parents can afford this. Or even if they're still alive. But I'm so pleased about getting rescued I can't even think about that.

If it turns out my parents never made it to Kingstown, we'll just have to give the sailors the slip. I don't know what we'll do after that, but it's bound to be better than getting hanged for piracy or going mad on a desert island and mistaking coconut shells for treasure.

George has put herself to work cleaning the decks and mending the sails. I would unleash my bilge water-carrying skills too, but their pump works fine.

George is pleased we're on the ship, but she gave me the side-eye when I told her I'd deliberately set my shelter on fire to get the attention of the ship.

It doesn't matter anymore. We've been rescued and it was all because of me, whether I did it on purpose or not.

Sunday, April 16th

We're closing in on Kingstown now. I've told George to make sure she never mentions anything about us being pirates. We'll be straight to the gallows if anyone finds out about that.

I'm really excited about returning to civilization, and I think George is too, even though she hasn't said much.

Maybe if things work out, I can arrange for her to live in Kingstown, too. She's saved my life quite a few times, so the least I can do is help her start a new life away from all the stinky sea rogues.

Monday, April 17th

We arrived at the docks this morning. I told the captain to wait on the ship and I'd return with his money, but he wasn't having it. He insisted two of his sailors accompany us to my dad's house.

George and I walked ahead, while the two sailors followed with their hands on the hilts of their cutlasses. Giving them the slip wasn't looking like an option. I just had to hope my parents had made it back. I hadn't survived storms, capture, and marooning just to get stabbed by angry sailors.

One of the locals pointed us in the direction of the governor's mansion. We strode down a dusty street flanked by carpenters, blacksmiths, and churches.

At the end of the street was a tall white building. We stepped up to the front door and knocked.

A woman in a pale blue dress answered.

"I'm here to see the governor," I said.

"He's busy," she said. "I could try and get you an appointment if you like."

"It's urgent," I said. I tried to think of a way to say the next part that wouldn't make me sound crazy. "I think I might be his son."

"He has no son," she said. "His son was lost at sea."

My heart leapt. Dad must have thought I'd been killed by the pirates when they took over our ship. This was going to be the best surprise ever for him.

"No he wasn't," I said. "I wasn't, I mean. It's me!"

The woman peered at me for a moment before wandering off into the dark hallway.

I heard her opening another door and murmuring.

A horrible thought struck me. What if the governor wasn't my dad at all, but someone who'd actually lost their son at sea? I'd look like the worst practical joker of all time. And the governor of a town wasn't a good person to get on the wrong side of.

The woman was coming back. There was somebody with her.

It was Dad. So that rickety old pirate ship had made it back to shore after all.

Dad glanced at me and scowled.

"Just as I thought," he said. "Some street urchin trying his luck."

"No!" I shouted. "It's me!" I ran my hands down my face, wiping away some of the dirt. Since dad had last seen me, I'd become coated with layers of grime, my hair had grown long and straggly, and my skin had reddened in the sun. It's no wonder he didn't recognize me.

Dad stepped forward and placed his hands on my shoulders.

"Thomas?" he asked. "Is that really you? I thought we'd lost you in the pirate attack."

"They kidnapped me," I said. I heard George tutting behind me. "But I managed to fight my way to freedom. With the help of my friend George here."

I turned to look at George, who was scowling. I don't think she was pleased with my white lie about the pirates taking me against my will. But I was hardly going to admit I'd chosen to become one. Dad would confine me to my room for ten years if he discovered that.

Tuesday, April 18ᵗʰ
Dad took me inside to meet Mom, who cried for about an hour. They were happy to pay

the reward to the sailors, and they'd probably have forked out even more.

So after all that time at sea, I'm now settling down in an actual house. And guess what? George is too. Mom and Dad were so impressed to hear how she'd saved my life, they offered to let her stay. She's been given her own room down the corridor from mine.

Even better, she's going to get a proper dress tomorrow. I can't wait to see her face when she finds out she's going to become a civilized lady.

Wednesday, April 19th

A dressmaker called Frances came round this morning to measure George.

George went bright red while Mom and Frances fussed around her and made her stand up straight. She didn't look as overjoyed as I'd hoped, but I'm sure she'll appreciate it when the dress is finished.

Mom has already given her a pair of shoes, and she's stomping up and down the corridor now to get used to them. It's as weird for her to walk in heels as it was for me to walk on the swaying ship when we first set sail.

Thursday, April 20th

George joined us for dinner this evening. Our chef served fish, and George grabbed it with both hands as if we were still on the desert island.

Mom showed her how to use her knife and fork. George still wolfed down the food too fast and rushed away without asking to be excused, but I'm sure she'll become more civilized soon. One step at a time.

Friday, April 21ˢᵗ

I spent most of today showing George the books in Dad's study. She can't read or write yet, but she's very curious and I think she'll be a quick learner. I wish I had some of my old fairy tale books to help her. The only things we have here are the Bible and Dad's law books, and they're very difficult to read.

George's dress was finished this afternoon and she wore it to dinner. She sat down quietly and ate with cutlery while Dad talked about his business in the town. You'd never guess she'd spent her life running around in filthy clothes and no shoes until just a few days ago.

Saturday, April 22nd

I went down to the docks with George today to look at the ships. Tiny rowing boats and single-masted sloops were bobbing around the big merchant vessels.

We spotted the boat that had rescued us from the desert island, and the crew waved at us.

I told George I'd enjoyed my time at sea, but I was glad to be back on land again. Being a pirate was quite an experience, but I didn't regret leaving that dangerous life behind.

I went back to the house, but George said she wanted to stay and look at the docks a little longer.

Sunday, April 23rd

I was woken by footsteps in the hallway early this morning. I thought we might have robbers, but when I opened the door I saw a small figure creeping around.

It was George, and she was back in her old clothes.

She spotted me and dashed out the front door.

I caught up with her on the street outside.

"I'm sorry," she said. "But the crew of the merchant ship has agreed to take me on as a deck cleaner. We leave at dawn."

"You don't need to scrub decks anymore," I said. "We're going to teach you to be civilized."

George sighed and looked down at her bare feet.

"I could no more survive in a place like this than you could on a desert island," she said. "I belong at sea."

"I was fine on the island," I said. "I'd have got the hang of fishing eventually."

George skulked off down the road. I paced after her and offered to fetch her dress and shoes, but she said she wouldn't need them.

She said she hopes to end up on another pirate ship, and she still wants to captain one eventually. I thought getting captured by the navy and almost hanged would have put her off, but it's only made her more determined. I really hope she doesn't end up dancing the hempen

jig somewhere. But she loves being a pirate
so much she's prepared to take the risk, and I
couldn't change her mind.

I watched George board the ship as the first
streaks of light were appearing in the sky. She
waved as they set off, then turned to face the
open sea.

The End

A History of Pirates

Thomas's diary was written in the early 18th century, at a time when piracy was rife in the Caribbean. This may have been the classic pirate era, but sea robbers have been around throughout history.

There are records of pirates in ancient Greece. They would sail around the Aegean Sea, attacking trade ships and ports. As well as stealing valuable goods, they would take prisoners to sell as slaves.

The Romans also suffered the same problem. Julius Caesar was kidnapped by pirates around 75 BC, but they released him for a ransom. He took his revenge by tracking them down and killing them. It was an

early sign of the ruthless leader he was
to become.

Scandinavian seafarers attacked merchant
ships and villages from the 8th century to
the 11th century. They're better known as
Vikings, but they also were a type of pirate.

In the Middle Ages, some countries began
to use pirates to attack their enemies.
They became known as privateers. King
Henry III of England used them against
the French in the 13th century, allowing
some crews a "letter of marque" that gave
them the right to plunder other ships.
Privateers flourished when Spanish ships
gathered treasure from the "New World"
of North and South America from the
16th century. Sailors like Sir Francis Drake

traveled to the Spanish Main to prey on them. The association of pirates and treasure stuck, even though most of them pursued much less exciting things, as Thomas found.

King James I tried to call an end to privateering in 1603 by withdrawing all letters of marque, but many continued attacking ships anyway.

Early on, Thomas meets Samuel, a pirate who escaped slavery. The Transatlantic Slave Trade was a dark period in world history that lasted from the 16th to the 19th century. During this time, between 10 million and 12 million Africans were captured, forced onto ships, and sold into slavery. Slave ships were overcrowded and unsanitary, and the treatment of enslaved people was brutal and inhumane.

Throughout the 17th and 18th centuries, pirates plundered merchant ships in the Caribbean. This is the era most people think of when they hear the word pirate today. However, as Thomas discovered, pirates were ruthless criminals with little in common with the jolly figures of legend.

Many popular myths about pirates come from books such as *Treasure Island* by Robert Louis Stevenson, which featured Long John Silver. Further characters such as Captain Hook from *Peter Pan* and Captain Jack Sparrow from the film series *Pirates of the Caribbean* also have shaped our notions. Far removed from these fun adventure stories, piracy continues today. In areas such as East Asia, boats carrying valuable items often are attacked by robbers. Life for these modern pirates is dangerous and brutal, just as it has been for pirates in every age.

How Do We Know About Pirates?

A large amount of evidence from the classic era of piracy survives. There are journals written by people who sailed with them. There are countless maps, records, codes of conduct, and official documents such as the letters of marque issued by kings. Objects like compasses, telescopes, and weapons can teach us about this time, too.

Much of our information about pirates in the 17th and 18th centuries comes from books that were published at the time. One of the most famous is called *A General History of the Robberies and Murders of the Most Notorious Pyrates*, which was published in 1724. It contained biographies of famous figures such as Blackbeard, Calico Jack, and Anne Bonny.

The book influenced authors like J.M. Barrie and Robert Louis Stevenson, and played a huge part in shaping our ideas about sea robbers. When studying a document like this, we have to work out which parts are true and which parts were exaggerated to make the stories more exciting.

Timeline

Around 500 BC

Pirate attacks are common around the Greek islands during this time. Ships carrying precious cargoes of tin, silver, copper, and amber are targeted.

67 BC

When pirates steal Roman grain supplies, Pompey the Great wages war on them. Many are wiped out, but the problem doesn't go away for long.

AD 793

Vikings destroy the abbey of Lindisfarne off the northeast coast of England. This often is seen as the start of the Viking era. The Norse seafarers would plunder ships and villages for the next three centuries.

Around 1100

Pirates from the Barbary Coast of Africa plunder trade vessels in the Mediterranean.

Timeline

1243

King Henry III gives some sailors permission to target enemies in return for a share of the profits. This begins the era of the privateer, when pirates are authorized to attack certain ships.

1492

Christopher Columbus sails to the West Indies. Soon, Spanish ships are voyaging to the New World to grab treasure, and pirates are preying on them.

1562

The privateer John Hawkins captures three hundred African people to sell in the Caribbean. The slave trade is a profitable business, but the enslaved people suffer horrific cruelty. Some escape and end up on pirate ships.

Timeline

1603

King James I tries to outlaw privateers, but many carry on pirate activity without his permission.

1630s

Criminals known as buccaneers are driven off the island of Hispaniola by the Spanish. They become pirates, looting merchant ships.

1704

Alexander Selkirk is stranded on a desert island off the coast of Chile. He manages to survive until he's rescued over four years later. The idea of a castaway living on a desert island soon grabs the imagination of the public.

1718

The notorious pirate Edward "Blackbeard" Teach is defeated by the British navy at the Ocracoke Inlet, off the coast of North Carolina.

208

Timeline

1724
The book *A General History of the Robberies and Murders of the Most Notorious Pyrates* is published. It stirs up interest in pirates and inspires many more books.

1883
Treasure Island by Robert Louis Stevenson is published. It has a massive influence on the way the public thinks about pirates.

2009
The cargo ship *Maersk Alabama* is hijacked by Somali pirates in the Indian Ocean. This event inspired the 2013 film *Captain Phillips*, starring Tom Hanks and Barkhad Abdi, which drew attention to piracy in the modern era.

Pirate Hall of Fame

Sea robbers have been around throughout history, but the most famous pirates come from the 16th, 17th, and 18th centuries. Here are the ocean-faring rogues whose names live on today.

Sir Francis Drake (c.1540-1596)

Sir Francis Drake was an English privateer who was permitted to attack Spanish ships by Queen Elizabeth I. He sailed around the world between 1577 and 1580, capturing a huge cargo of treasure along the way. He was knighted soon after his return.

Henry Morgan (c.1635-1688)

Henry Morgan was a Welsh seafarer who started out as a privateer. His crew captured Panama City in 1671, an amazing achievement for a gang of outlaws rather than an official army.

Pirate Hall of Fame

Francois L'Olonnais (c.1635-c.1668)

Francois L'Olonnais was a French pirate who forged a reputation for nastiness and struck fear into his enemies. According to 17th century author Alexander Exquemelin, L'Olonnais once cut out a victim's heart and ate it in front of another prisoner.

Edward Teach (1680-1718)

Known as "Blackbeard," Edward Teach made himself look frightening by tying ribbons into his beard and wearing a sling of pistols over his shoulder. He was even known to have twisted burning ropes into his hair. He is believed to have killed his own crew members just for fun.

Bartholomew Roberts (c.1682-1722)

Also known as "Black Bart," Bartholomew Roberts was one of the most successful pirates of all. He captured hundreds of ships in the

Pirate Hall of Fame

early 18th century. Unusually for a pirate, he didn't drink, and he hated gambling and smoking. Roberts made his crews follow strict rules like turning off lights and candles at eight o'clock at night.

Ned Low (c.1690 - c.1724)

A notoriously violent English pirate who had a reputation for torturing his victims. According to reports, he sliced off his enemies' ears and noses and set fire to their hands and feet.

Anne Bonny (c.1700 - c.1782)

Anne Bonny was a female seafarer who served on the ship of her boyfriend, Calico Jack. Also on the crew was another famous female pirate Mary Read. Biographies of both were included in the 1724 book *A General History of the Robberies and Murders of the Most Notorious Pyrates*.

Pirate Hall of Fame

John Rackham (1682-1720)

Better known as "Calico Jack," John Rackham operated in the Caribbean in the early 18th century. His flag of a skull and two crossed swords is still commonly used as a symbol of piracy today. When Calico Jack's ship was attacked by the British navy in 1720, he supposedly hid in the hold while his female crew members, Anne Bonny and Mary Read, went out to fight.

Long John Silver

Okay, he wasn't real. But the villain of Robert Louis Stevenson's *Treasure Island* has done more than any genuine person to fix our notions of pirates. He has a pet parrot who perches on his shoulder and repeats the words "Pieces of eight," he uses phrases like "Shiver me timbers," and he loves treasure. Pirate costumes in fancy dress shops are greatly influenced by film portrayals of this character.

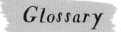

Glossary

Bilge
The bottom part of the inside of a ship. The water that collected here was removed by a pump or with a bucket.

Bow
The front of a ship.

Buccaneer
This name originally referred to pirates from the island of Hispaniola in the 17th century, but became a general term for pirates.

Caltrops
Metal spikes designed to always land with a spike facing up. They were used as weapons against barefooted pirates.

Cat-O'-Nine-Tails
A whip with nine strands on the end used to punish those who'd broken the rules.

Corsair
A name given to pirates from the Barbary Coast of North Africa who plundered ships in the Mediterranean.

Cutlass
A sword with a short, broad blade that was easy to wield in crowded battles.

Dock
A place on the coast where ships stop for cargo and passengers.

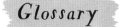

Glossary

Galley
The kitchen of a ship. The word also can refer to a type of ship powered by rowers.

Grog
A mixture of rum and water drunk by sailors.

Hardtack
A cheap long-lasting type of biscuit that was popular on ships.

Jolly Roger
The name for a pirate's flag. The most famous ones are the skull and crossbones and the skull and crossed swords, but in practice, every pirate had their own unique design.

Keelhauling
The punishment of being dragged across the rough underside of a ship. This could happen while a ship was run up on a beach, but sometimes it was done underwater for extra horribleness.

Marooning
A punishment where a pirate would be left on a desert island to die alone.

Mast
Tall poles that rise vertically from ships.

Moses' Law
The belief that a victim should be given thirty-nine lashes with a whip, as any more could be fatal. Of course, in reality any number of lashes can kill someone.

Glossary

Pieces of Eight
A silver coin, worth eight reales, which was an old Spanish unit of currency.

Port
The left side of a ship if you're facing forward.

Privateer
Seafarers who have been granted the right to attack and plunder ships by a government.

Scurvy
A disease caused by a lack of vitamin C. It was common in pirates who ate no fruits or vegetables.

Sloop
A small sailing ship with a single mast.

Some pirates used these for hiding in narrow inlets where bigger ships couldn't follow.

Starboard
The right side of a ship if you're facing forward.

Stern
The rear of a ship.

Topsails
Square sails set above the lowest sails.

Yard
The horizontal pole of wood fixed to a mast to support sails.